Max Evan and Maria Evan

In The Land of Broken Time

Published 2017

In The Land of Broken Time

Authors Max Evan and Maria Evan.
Illustrator Maria Evan.
Translator Helen Hagon.

In The Land of Broken Time

Contents

Chapter 1
How Christopher and Sophie Became Hijackers

Since early in the morning, this summer's day had turned out to be quite different from the rest. Scarcely had Christopher gone down to breakfast when there was a long beep from outside, followed by another, and then a third…The boy rushed over to the window and saw a line of huge trucks driving past his house. They were brightly painted and glittered in the light of the rising sun.

"The circus!" Christopher exclaimed.

"A traveling circus, with a Big Top," his mother explained.

She was pouring delicious cocoa into cups. The boy ran out into the meadow.

"This evening and all week! An unforgettable show!" a voice said from a loudspeaker.

"Mum! Mum, can we go?!" the boy began to shout.

"Well, not today. And don't forget we have to go to the doctor tomorrow."

For the whole of the previous week, Christopher had been forced to stay at home because he had a cold. He had spent the first two days in bed, and the time had passed incredibly slowly. But then he had started to improve. Time began to speed up.

"But I'm better now!"

"Perhaps," his mother objected, "but only the doctor can say whether you have fully recovered or not."

Christopher watched sadly as the trucks moved away. He really, really wanted to watch the amazing show, even from a distance. He felt like running after it.

As evening approached, Christopher sat by the window and watched whole processions of excited children walking past. They were hurrying to the suburbs in the northern part of the town. A huge dome had been erected on some wasteland there. Christopher could see the top of it from upstairs. The sound of cheerful music came from far away. Apparently the festivities were in full swing, and the main performance was due to begin soon.

The boy so wished he could at least catch a glimpse of it all…*We've already had supper*, he thought. *So no one will miss me before bedtime. I'll run there and then straight back again.*

Escaping from the house without being noticed wasn't too difficult; Dad was watching the news on the computer in his study, and Mum was studying new recipes on her tablet in the living room. They were both so absorbed in what they were doing that neither of them noticed the fugitive slipping out. Christopher knew that running away was wrong, but his legs carried him off, all by themselves.

He shot like a bullet along the streets and soon reached his destination.

A huge balloon was being blown up next to the Big Top. The shaped fabric was rapidly filling up with helium. Soon it began to sway from side to side. It was fastened to the ground with a rope.

The third and final bell sounded to indicate that the performance was about to start, and everyone hurried inside. Christopher didn't have a ticket, though.

He tried to hide in the crowd so that, in the general chaos, he might be able to sneak into the kingdom of clowns and acrobats. A steward dressed in uniform was struggling to check all the tickets. The boy had almost managed to squeeze himself through the forbidden doorway when a loud and piercing voice screamed over the general hubbub:

"Look! He hasn't got a ticket!"

Christopher's heart sank. The steward looked at the boy and was about to grab hold of him. But help arrived from a rather unexpected source. A girl, who was standing just behind him, pointed in the opposite direction and shouted loudly:

"Look! What's that?!"

Everyone turned in the direction she was pointing. Making the most of this, the cunning girl lifted up the curtain without a second's delay and slipped inside. Then she grabbed hold of Christopher and dragged him in behind her. He found this boldness rather awkward at first, and he even tried to object, but then he realized why the girl had done it. She had no ticket, either! Everything had happened so quickly that, when the curtain fell back into place, hiding the young conspirators, he stood for a moment peering through to the other side in confusion.

"Ssshhh!" the girl whispered.

"We'll be caught," Christopher said quietly.

"But we'll get to see the show!" she declared confidently. "Are you coming?"

They were about the same age, and Christopher didn't want his new friend to think he was a coward. The boy darted past the girl, grabbed her by the hand, and pulled her after him. His knees were trembling slightly with nerves.

"I'm called Sophie," she said, introducing herself as they made their way through a messy heap of boxes.

"I'm Christopher."

Everything smelled of leather and hay. They managed to reach the curtain, behind which was the stage. Pulling it back carefully, they peered through the gap, their heads almost touching. The show had already started, and the children soon forgot about everything else in the world.

It was an amazing sight to see. Some jugglers were performing, throwing white, oval-shaped, egg-like objects to each other. For the grand finale, a performer in a striped body suit tossed the objects high into the air, one by one. A gasp of amazement filled the whole room. The eggs broke with a loud crack, and a parrot flew out of each one.

"I'm going to sweep you up!" a voice croaked from behind them.

The children turned around. It was an old woman who looked a lot like a witch. She was even holding the handle of a broom. Locks of tangled grey hair fell from her head over her forehead and down to her shoulders. A dark eye twinkled maliciously. Christopher's legs felt as if they had stopped obeying him. He glanced at the girl and saw that she was frightened, too.

"Run!" Christopher said in a voice that could barely be heard, and then he took Sophie by the hand.

The children moved slowly at first, creeping step by step past the curtain, and when they had summoned up the courage, they ran as fast as their legs would carry them.

"Stop! Where are you going!" the old woman called, smiling and hobbling after them.

She wasn't a witch at all, of course, but was just making sure everything was kept neat and tidy. However, neither Christopher nor Sophie realized that. They ran outside.

In front of them was a deserted area. In the middle, the balloon was still swaying.

"Let's hide in the basket!" the girl suggested.

She climbed first into the wicker container and waved over the edge. Christopher hesitated only for a moment. The children dropped down to the bottom and hid there. From the direction of the circus, they could hear the clicking of footsteps and the swishing of a broom as it swept the ground. The old woman was muttering something under her breath.

It must be some kind of curse, Sophie thought, while Christopher looked around. Directly above his head was the end of the rope that was fastening the balloon to the ground. He supposed that, to untie the knot, all he would have to do would be to pull the rope. The girl looked at him. They both realized in horror that they had been caught in a trap. The witch would be sure to find them! They could already hear her wheezing, groaning and shuffling her feet as she moved closer and closer.

Christopher grabbed the rope. After a moment's hesitation, Sophie did the same.

"There you are!" a voice said from directly above them. "Now I'm going to make you muck out the elephants' pen!"

The children grimaced and pulled the cable with all their might. The knot came undone, and the balloon shot straight upward.

"Wait! Where are you going, my dears!" the witch cried from down below, but there was nothing to be done. The balloon soared up high and, caught by the wind, began to sail over the town.

Christopher and Sophie peered out from inside the basket. The witch had dropped her broom and was holding her head in both hands, giving the impression that something disastrous had happened. A few more people who weren't taking part in the show ran out of the circus tent, but all they could do was follow the balloon with their eyes as it floated away.

Down to the left, the children could see houses, and to the right there were green fields beyond the river, while in the distance, almost on the horizon, mountains rose. The air current was carrying the children in that direction.

"How are we going to get back now?" the girl asked anxiously.

"There must be a way," the boy replied.

They began to look around. A large pile of circus equipment— clothes, wigs, and all kinds of old props—had been left at the bottom of the basket. Christopher pulled a handle that was sticking out of the pile. It was a fine sword in a scabbard, on a leather belt with a bronze buckle. It was just the right size for the boy. Christopher looked at the sword in delight. He wasn't planning to steal it, of course. He was just going to hold it for a while.

The children went on rummaging through the objects, until they heard first a snore and then a snort.

"Someone's in there!" exclaimed Christopher. He froze, and Sophie bit her lip.

They carefully lifted a red elastic clown nose. Another nose poked out from underneath it, but this time it was a real one. It was black and wet with pale fur around it. It was a dog! Without opening its eyes, it yawned, revealing a row of big white teeth. The dog moved one ear from side to side, and only then did its eyelashes begin to flutter open.

"It's a Labrador," said Sophie. "They're nice."

"I'm not a Labrador. I'm a Retriever. And not an ordinary one, but a Golden Retriever," the dog said. "But I'm not vicious—you were right about that."

"A talking dog!" the children exclaimed.

The dog had a very noble appearance, with a round chest and smooth, shiny fur. It was a fine golden color, except for a pale, star-shaped patch, which was especially visible when it wagged its amber tail.

"Of course I can talk," replied the Retriever. "I'm not an ordinary dog. I'm a circus dog. My name's Duke."

"Christopher," the boy said, bowing his head.

He felt as if something was changing, both inside him and around him. The knightly sword at his side seemed to be making him act in an appropriate fashion for the situation, regal and confident.

"I'm Sophia, but you can call me Sophie, or just So."

"My ears are telling me we're flying somewhere."

"Yes, we're flying, but we don't know where to," the boy explained.

"How did you come to be here?" asked the girl.

"Oh, it's quite simple. I like to sleep in peace, but there's such a commotion in the circus when the show is on!" Duke stood up on his hind legs and they all looked down together. "I don't recognize this place."

The wind grew stronger. It became colder. Clouds appeared, and soon they were flying through a band of fog so thick that our heroes could hardly see each other.

"How can we steer the balloon?" asked the boy.

"It flies where the wind takes it. But it could land at any moment. Hold onto that string. It opens a valve up there," the dog said, wiggling his head. "The gas will start to escape, and we'll begin to descend."

"But we can't see what's down there," said Sophie. "There might be a river or a lake. Everyone agreed with this sensible thought. Already, Christopher could tell she had good sense. It was no wonder her name meant 'wise'. She, too, now felt as if the world around them was going through some mysterious changes, even though it was hidden beneath a band of fog.

A strong wind began to blow, and it swept the fog away. Steep cliffs rose up directly ahead of the young balloonists. It became obvious that if they didn't do something quickly, they would crash.

"Look out!" barked the retriever, grabbing the string with his teeth. They could neither see nor hear the valve opening at the top, but the balloon started to go down slowly. They landed in a wide valley surrounded by mountains on all sides.

The sides of the basket gently brushed against the green grass, and then it came to a halt. The dog leaped out first. He sniffed the ground and then raced off toward the forest. Duke's wonderful, bright amber tail flew over the grass with every energetic bound.

Chapter 2

In a Trap

"Everything smells different here," said Duke when he returned. "It's not the same as the place we came from. The grass, the dry twigs, the fallen leaves, even the earth that I dug up with my paws: everything has a slightly different scent. And then there's the forest! I ran along the edge of it—the trees are so close together, and vines grow around them. There are thorny bushes all over. Even when I crawled on my belly I couldn't get through!"

"So…have we been caught in a trap!?" exclaimed Sophia.

"There's no way out of here," said Christopher. "It's also strange that the sun is just as high as before, yet evening should have come ages ago. The circus performance started at eight. Adding on the time we have spent flying…It must be past 10 o'clock by now."

"Half past 10 at least," the dog stated. "That's feeding time at the circus, and my stomach is telling me that it needs refreshment."

Sophia pulled a packet of biscuits out of her pocket.

"Here, help yourselves."

The friends shared this modest supper, or perhaps, judging by the sun, it could have even been lunch. They looked at the forest where, in the darkness beneath the trees, some kind of lights were glimmering. It was probably fireflies buzzing about. Then, when the young travelers turned around, they cried out in surprise. The balloon, which had been lying on the grass like a huge prehistoric creature, had silently deflated. In the very middle of the meadow, they noticed a round disc.

"Oh my goodness!" exclaimed Christopher.

"Wow!" gasped Sophie.

"Woof!" yapped Duke.

"How come we didn't notice that from high up?" Sophie shouted as they ran toward the mysterious object.

Duke, of course, had run on ahead of them, so the question was directed at Christopher.

"You were so frightened that you closed your eyes, and I was busy watching you!"

"I wasn't frightened at all," replied Sophie. "The basket had started to spin, and I felt dizzy. That's why I closed my eyes."

"It looks like a flying saucer that has crashed!" the boy gasped, puffing and panting after running so fast. "Perhaps we're not the first to have landed in this meadow!"

As they ran closer, the children realized that it wasn't an alien ship at all. Bright yellow rays of light shone out from the central part of the disc. They were each drawn toward the numbers arranged like a necklace around the edge.

"It's a sundial," Sophie declared confidently.

"I can see that," Christopher retorted, "but there is no pole, or anything that might cast a shadow. It's useless. Or perhaps…"

He stepped carefully into the center. His shadow pointed to the number 13.

"The sun isn't moving!" he said, lost in thought.

"That's impossible!" Sophie and Duke called out in unison.

"It's true. See how my shadow is absolutely still. The light source mustn't be moving. If it really is our sun, that is, and not some other star."

"Wait a moment. Let's check to make sure," the girl suggested. "I'll stand right on top of the number 13 and see whether your shadow moves even just a millimeter."

However, the young explorers didn't have a chance to carry out their important experiment. Sophie stood with one leg on the number 1 and the other on the number 3, and invisible cogs immediately began to move under the ground. The earth itself shook so much that the children struggled to stay upright. They put their arms out to help them balance. Although the dog was still standing on all fours, he stuck out his tail, and the fur on his back stood on end.

The wind grew stronger. It blew on Christopher's back and Sophie's face. Running over to the girl, the dog pushed her off her feet. The boy raced over as well, and the three of them toppled head over heels onto the grass. At that very moment, lightning struck. A bright flash lit up everywhere around. A fiery bolt shot out of the sundial and toward the forest. It seemed as if the currents of scorching hot air, flying over the heads of the adventurers and leaving them sprawled on the ground, might burn every living thing in their path. But something quite different happened. The trees parted! Not one of them was harmed. In that same place where the trees had been so dense and impenetrable, there was now a wide path leading off into the depths of this mysterious land.

Maria Evan and Max Evan «In The Land of Broken Time»

Everything was silent. For a few minutes, they stared at each other in amazement.

Christopher was afraid. However, he tried not to show it, as he realized that Sophie was scared, too, so he had to keep everything calm.

"The sundial has shown us the way," Sophie eventually managed to say. "At least we're not stuck in this meadow any more."

"I've just remembered something! I have a phone," exclaimed the boy.

"And you've said nothing all this time!" the girl said in surprise as she glanced at the slender smartphone in Christopher's hand.

Meanwhile, he was wondering what he should do. On one hand, he ought to call his parents straight away. They would be worried. But then he would have to confess to running away, sneaking into the circus without a ticket, and then hijacking a hot air balloon. On the other hand, they might not yet have realized that he was gone. So maybe there was no need to phone them just yet...

No, not yet, he decided. That might make things worse.

Quick-witted Sophie helped put an end to his doubts.

"The telephone won't help us anyway," she said. "You see, there's no signal out here. We won't be able to make a call."

"That's true! We're surrounded by mountains. We're right at the bottom of a valley, and radio waves won't reach down here. We must go on further, and the signal should come back as we move higher up."

"We would do better to wait here next to the balloon," the girl objected. "People are bound to be looking for us, and the balloon is easy to spot."

"We'll leave a note, then," suggested the boy.

Their message read as follows:

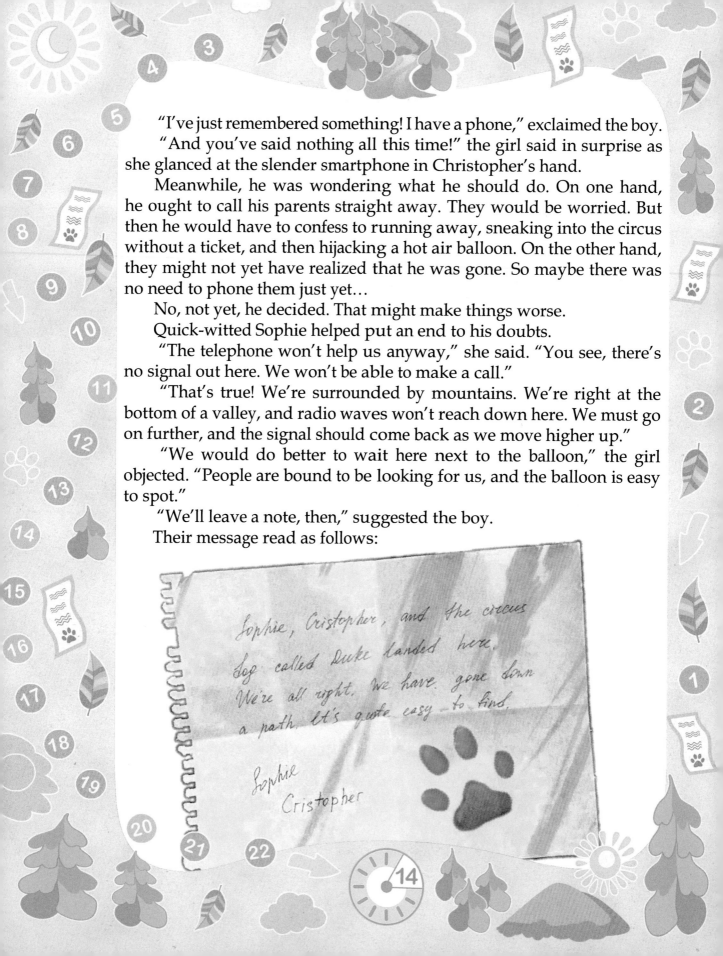

Sophie, Cristopher, and the circus dog called Duke landed here. We're all right. We have gone down a path. It's quite easy to find.

Sophie
Cristopher

The girl and boy scribbled their names on the scrap of paper, and the dog put his paw on it, leaving a muddy mark.

"Just a moment," Christopher said suddenly. "I have an idea."

He pulled out his smartphone again, and opened a map program.

"Now we'll be able to work out where we are. It works, even without the direct phone signal."

This explanation was for Duke's benefit. But apparently he didn't need it.

"My friend," the dog said, "our circus travels all over the world. There's a GPS device in every truck."

The tech-savvy retriever wagged his tail happily, and stuck his furry chest out even further. The sun's rays, which shone through the leaves, played on his glistening fur, making it look as if it were covered with gold medals.

"Look! Something's not quite right here," Sophie said as the app opened up.

There was a brightly colored spot on the map, showing where they were. They could see a green valley, with a river and many streams running through it. There were mountains around it, and lots of smaller details. However, there was nothing at all to be seen beyond the mountains, no matter how much Christopher zoomed in and out. The forest ahead of them was labeled "Forest of Chronos."

"I don't understand how this map got onto the phone at all," said the boy.

"It doesn't even look like a real place," the girl piped up. "This map is more like something out of a computer game. Are you playing tricks on us?!"

Christopher frowned. He was hurt by the suggestion that he might have altered the satellite image. In order to dispel all doubt, the young balloon thief marched straight off into the forest.

"Look!" he shouted to the others. "The spot is moving with me. That proves it's a real map of the area. It's a good thing we have it. Now we won't get lost!"

He tried to say this with confidence, to cheer up Sophie. Glancing at the balloon again, the girl reluctantly began to follow her new friend. The dog needed no persuasion. He set off running, and quickly caught up with the two-legged creatures. He promptly ran on ahead down the footpath, then came back, as if encouraging the travellers and telling them that the way was clear.

The light was dimmer under the trees, and the further they went, the darker it became. At first, the path wound amongst small cypress trees. Then fir trees with spreading branches began to appear. Duke, being a real guard dog, searched the bushes on both sides of the footpath. Suddenly, a sound like a raging torrent could be heard up ahead.

"It's a stream," the dog growled, pricking up his ears. "The wind is bringing me the scent of water and smoke."

Chapter 3

Four-Pointed Star on a Four-Legged Friend

A log cabin stood on the banks of the raging stream, thick smoke pouring out of its chimney.

"There are people in there," Sophie exclaimed. "They will help us to find the way home."

A rather elderly but agile man of medium height, wearing a tattered leather hat and an apron, came running out of the house. Dangling on his chest was a pince-nez. A kind smile played on his lips, while the wrinkles at the corners of his eyes were like rays of starlight. His left hand was also covered with wrinkles.

The stranger was extremely busy. Without noticing anything around him, he went over to the window first, and pulled a thin cable through it. He then pulled another one from a contraption in a lean-to in front of the house. It was an hourglass, which had been mounted in such a way that it could be turned over vertically. If you pulled the rope, it would flip over and begin to measure time. A similar hourglass could be seen inside the house, too. It must have been very hot in there, because there was steam coming out of the window.

"One, two, three," the odd gentleman counted, and then he tugged both ropes. The hourglasses turned at the same time. The sand inside trickled downwards. The experimenter feasted his eyes on the timepieces. He even crouched down in his enthusiasm, so that he didn't miss anything. When the last grain of sand in the outdoor hourglass had joined the other thousands of pale yellow particles just like it, the sand in the indoor one was still falling.

"It has been measured…in the cold and in the warm," the stranger chattered bafflingly. "So, it must be lighter in the cold!"

He jumped up and down with excitement, and only then did he notice the children. He didn't seem at all surprised at their appearance, or by the dog next to them. What did it matter if there were boys and girls traveling around the world with their dogs?

17

"The clocks are absolutely identical," he went on, unperturbed. On one hand, he seemed to be talking to the children, but on the other he appeared to be telling himself about the experiment. "I blew the glass containers myself. And they contain exactly the same amount of sand. Each one has one-and-a-half million particles of sand: grain for grain. I even have a certificate from the Ant Queen. Her subjects counted them."

"From the Ant Queen?" the children exclaimed together, and only then did the man take a closer look at them.

"Of course." He showed them a piece of paper with uneven edges and print. "Who else but ants could accurately count such a large quantity? Allow me to introduce myself: Temporus Certus, natural experimenter and professor of the 'Knowledge of Ignorance' faculty at the university of Knowitall. And you?"

"My name is Christopher, this is Sophia, and this is Duke," the boy told him. "We flew here in a hot air balloon from Richmond Hill."

"Richmond Hill…Never heard of it. And where is your balloon?"

"We left it in the field. Near the sundial."

"You saw the sundial and you're still alive?" the professor said, his eyes wide with surprise. "I hope you didn't attempt to use it to tell the time."

The children fell into an awkward silence, not knowing how to respond.

"I see that you did," the scientist said, clutching the back of his head. His hat flew off onto the ground, but he didn't even notice.

"We're trying to find our way home," Sophie commented, picking up the hat and politely offering it back to the professor. "We need to get to the mountains. We saw them from the air. They're over in that direction."

"Forget about that!" the professor replied, lowering his voice. "Crossing the stream is dangerous. And as for going through the mountains—don't even think about it! I've never seen anyone bold enough in all my born days, and I don't advise you to try it."

At that moment, he noticed the sword on Christopher's belt, faltered for a moment, and then went on enthusiastically:

"How unobservant I am! A boy and a girl, with a sword and a dog!"

Duke immediately pulled a serious face and stuck out his chest.

"Such pedigree! That's quite obvious. Absolutely! Once again, everything has been made clear for us. I see that you are frowning, my four-legged friend, because I grouped you together with a sword—an inanimate object. However, I did that because you have something special in common. A sword is a magical thing. And you, too, are not as simple as you seem. If I am not mistaken, there should be a star-shaped mark right next to your tail. Is that true?"

This made Duke even more troubled. Firstly, how could he be magical? What was this all about? Yes, he was a circus dog, but was he really magical? He had seen magicians in the circus, and he knew all their tricks by heart. It was pure sleight of hand. Secondly, the dog was embarrassed by his mark. For as long as he could remember, his fur had been golden and his tail amber, but that patch next to his tail spoiled it all. It was white. It would have been another matter entirely if the mark had been on his chest. That would have been something to be proud of. But it was not the same at all when it was in quite the opposite place.

"That's not just a mark," Temporus Certus went on. "It's a sign to show that you are special."

The professor bowed to Duke, and the dog began to realize that the scientist wasn't trying to offend him at all. He turned around reluctantly.

"In fact, it is a four-pointed star on a four-legged friend!" the professor shouted, and then ran into the house.

From inside came the sound of hinges scraping, and the clanging of pots being tossed about. A moment later their new friend peered out of the window and called to them all to come inside.

In the room that served as both an office and a laboratory, it was even hotter still. All over, there were shelves with flasks. The cupboard contained scrolls of parchment. A stuffed parrot sat in an enormous cage.

"Now. It's here somewhere!" Their new friend unrolled one of the scrolls onto the table. "It says here that that the three will appear when the time is near. One of them will have a sword. Young man, would you mind removing the weapon from its sheath?"

Christopher carefully took out the sword, and the children gasped in unison. The steel, which had been dull before, now had a faint, bluish glow.

"The closer you are to the target, the brighter the blade will become. Its light will change from pale blue to bright red."

"The closer you are to what target?" asked the boy.

"It doesn't say in the text. It is only known that a prince and his companions will save our land from the misfortune which has befallen it. Oh yes! I quite forgot."

He ran off into the next room, then returned holding something in his clenched fist. Barely able to conceal his excitement, he unfurled his fingers. Something bright and sparkling darted out of his hand. It was a necklace with a pendant. It hovered in the air, sending a shower of red and yellow all around. Then it moved in a semicircle around the room, came to a halt right in front of the girl, and, a second later, put itself around her neck!

The children gave another surprised shriek.

"It's magic" gasped the girl.

"It is yours," the scientist told her.

Everyone watched in amazement. The pendant was a large, precious stone. Sophie thanked the professor. She held the stone closer to her eyes. Her breath touched its surface and then another miracle happened. The cold fire around the stone flickered, as if blown by the wind, causing individual flames to flare up, drawing mysterious symbols in the air.

A low voice, which sounded as if it was coming from thousand-year-old depths, spoke, stretching out each syllable:

"Into town a prince shall come,
And with him his two friends.
They will find the way back home:
That's where their journey ends."

Chapter 4
Fish that Never Grow Old

The voice fell silent. Then the light faded, too.

"What does it mean?!" Sophie asked.

"The pendant is prompting you. Always carry it with you. In a moment of need, like now, your breath will bring the stone to life."

"Only in a moment of need? Can't the necklace just tell us how to get home?" There was disappointment in Sophie's voice.

"Everything in its own time. You should go to the capital. That was clearly what the necklace was telling you."

"And what kind of problems might there be?" Christopher enquired matter-of-factly.

"All sorts," sighed the professor. "But they are all linked to the incorrect passage of time. Sometimes it speeds up, and sometimes it slows down. It jumps about, creating chaos and confusion. My experiments are connected with this. I seem to have found a possible cause—the surrounding temperature. The higher it is, the slower time passes. It's still only a theory, but it has already been strengthened by today's experiment!"

"And who can deal with these problems?" the boy asked again.

"The matter is of great interest to Temporus Improbus. He is my brother. We have been arguing for many years. We began our research together, but I must say that he went much further with his experiments and, according to the rumors, he achieved remarkable successes. Since then, though, all kinds of bad things have been happening here."

Sophia whispered something into Christopher's ear, and then said aloud:

"Of course, we don't mind saving your land from suffering and misfortune, if that is what the ancient legends say. But our parents will probably already have noticed that we are gone, and will have started to panic. When my mother is nervous, everyone else has to keep still and avoid any sudden movements. Otherwise, there will be trouble. We need to go home. So if crossing the stream is dangerous, then perhaps you could show us a different way to get to the town."

"There is one way. And you won't have to go through the Forest of Chronos."

He dashed out of the house, ran over to the water, dipped his foot into the river sand three times, and then ran straight back.

"Where on earth are you?" his voice called out from the room next door.

Meanwhile, a fish poked its pointed nose out of the river.

"Here it is. Take this!" the professor said, returning to the children with a nightcap in his hand, and offering it to Christopher.

"Thank you, but I'm used to sleeping without anything on my head," the boy replied politely.

A sword on my belt is one thing, he thought, but a ridiculous, pointy, white cloth hat is quite different.

"I'm not wearing it, either," Sophie said, grimacing.

"Nor me," barked the dog.

"Wait a moment!" the professor said, raising his index finger. "This cap isn't for sleeping. It is for a duel. On the other side of the Chronos stream is the Forest of Chronos—a huge bamboo forest which is so old that it seems as if it has been around forever. In there, many dangers await travellers. You will have to make a detour, first of all across the water, and then along the railway. It's not too difficult. I'll give you a boat. That will make it easy for you to get to the Coalless and Steamless railway station. Persicus, the sturgeon, is an old friend of mine. He will take you upstream. All you need to do when you reach the appointed place is to throw him a line—the thin rope attached to the front of the boat. Afterward, he will bring my boat back to me safe and sound."

"Do you mean to say that he will pull the boat against the current?" the boy asked doubtfully.

"Sturgeon are strong fish. They don't grow old, either. Never," the scientist added for some reason. "That, you will soon see in these parts, is a very important quality."

He rubbed the wrinkled palm of his left hand with his perfectly smooth right one.

"But what should we do about tickets for the train?" asked Sophie. "And what time is the one we need to catch?"

"Ah, my dear creatures. There have been no tickets for a long time, just as there is no timetable. When all this trouble began with the time, the trains stopped running. Do I really need to tell you how important punctuality is in these circumstances? When you don't know what will happen to the time along the way, or what kind of rail connections there are. The trains are running now. From time to time, but not on time. You will have to hijack one."

"Hijack?!" yelped the dog. "I've spent my whole life catching thieves in the circus. I can't allow a theft to be carried out right under my nose, and certainly can't participate in one!"

"I see that you are not only an intelligent dog, but also a noble one," replied Temporus Certus. "You will not have to steal anything. Merula, the black gnome, looks after the railway station. He used to work as a fireman, and that is why he turned black. Now he lives permanently in an engine cab. It's daytime today, which means that Merula will be sleeping in the coal box. It is extremely dark inside there, so it's very important to find the rascal quickly and put the cap on him. Otherwise, he might whack you with a shovel. Gnomes' jokes are not funny. That's just their nature."

The children held their breath as they listened. Meanwhile, the scientist went on:

"Our fire-gnome has gone quite deaf from the constant blasts on the train's whistle directly above his ears, so it won't be too difficult to get close to him, as long as you act quickly, of course. He won't hear you, but he will certainly see you. It will be rather like a duel: one on one. This is no ordinary cap, but a magic one. It has a calming effect on the inhabitants of the underground kingdom. All their natural malice goes away, no matter who they are. Then it becomes possible to talk to them. Otherwise, these cave and pit dwellers are simply unbearable. It's quite complicated, so if you don't feel ready…"

"I'm ready," the boy said, taking a step forward.

"Excellent! Here you are."

The preparations for the journey didn't take long. Just a few minutes later, the children and the dog were sitting in a lovely boat, which was being slowly carried along with the current. Persicus was splashing about in the water a little way ahead. The professor had warned them that, just like all fish, this one was deaf. But he understood everything perfectly.

"Let me give you one final piece of advice, my brave young friend," Temporus Certus called to Christopher when the boat was already gliding over the smooth water of the river. "Before you go in to find the Black Gnome, close one eye for a couple of minutes. Then, when you push the door ajar and run into his hidey-hole, open your eye and spring into action."

"But how will that help?!" the boy cried.

The boat had sailed even further away by that point.

"You'll see," the children heard, and then, almost straight away, the house and the scientist disappeared around a bend.

Maria Evan and Max Evan «In The Land of Broken Time»

Chapter 5
Gnome with a Dubious Reputation

In spite of the fact that Persicus was the kind of fish that lived at the bottom of the river, he would swim up to the surface from time to time, look at the children, and then plunge back down again into the water.

"I've heard that sturgeon don't grow old at all," the boy said.

"That's not always the case," the circus dog remarked knowledgeably. "But our Persicus here seems to be one who hasn't. It feels like he's watching us mortals with those intense, glassy eyes."

"The professor said that not becoming older is very important around here," said Sophie. "Can time really move faster in this place?"

"If it can," objected Christopher, "then why didn't he just tell us so?"

"Did you see his left hand? It was all wrinkly, like an old man's. Perhaps it's the result of a time experiment that went wrong."

Christopher cringed. He remembered how he had often used to wish he could grow up faster. But to become old straight away would be simply awful!

Sophie was clearly thinking about the same thing. She leaned over the edge of the boat, carefully examined her reflection in the water, and let out a sigh of relief, as she hadn't noticed any changes.

Meanwhile, the river turned around a bend, becoming deeper all the time. The Forest of Chronos was behind them. Now there were just a few bushes growing on the right bank. Sounds of anxious clucking, happy grunting, and the occasional harmonious whistling were coming from over there. Duke pricked up his ears and sniffed at every noise. Then he began to close his eyes at intervals. Looking into the bright light wasn't very pleasant, even after a minute's break.

"Some kind of nonsense," the dog muttered quietly at last.

The railway station appeared around the next bend. It really did seem to be deserted. The paint on the buildings was peeling, and the bronze bell was covered with dust. The wind was blowing a few pieces of paper along the platform. The boy picked one of them up. It was a leaflet about some escaped criminals. Beneath the word 'Wanted' in big bold letters, it said:

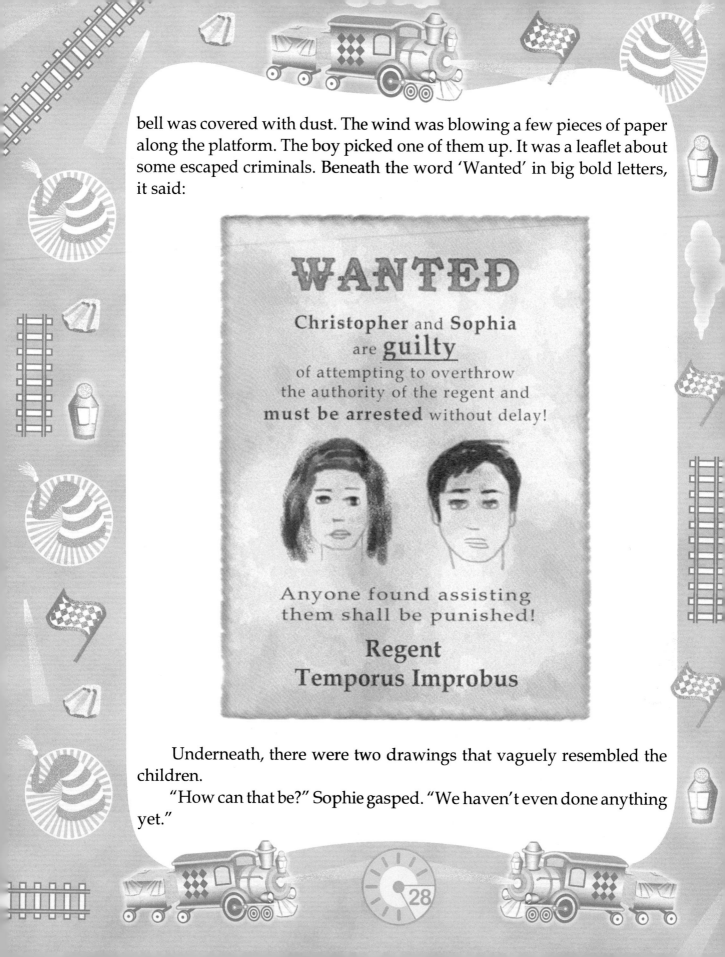

WANTED

Christopher and Sophia
are <u>guilty</u>
of attempting to overthrow
the authority of the regent and
must be arrested without delay!

Anyone found assisting
them shall be punished!

Regent
Temporus Improbus

Underneath, there were two drawings that vaguely resembled the children.

"How can that be?" Sophie gasped. "We haven't even done anything yet."

"But we set some kind of secret mechanism going with the sundial," said Christopher. "Perhaps that's what they mean by attempting to overthrow authority."

"The professor should have told us about it," Sophie replied with a shrug. "He was surprised that we were still alive."

"It turns out that the professor's brother has become some kind of important bigwig. He's the Regent now!"

"We haven't found the prince or princess yet—the real rulers. So is he in charge?"

"Well, no prince, anyway," the boy corrected. "What does a princess have to do with this? The legend doesn't mention her."

The girl deliberately pouted to show that she didn't agree with this version of things. Instead of arguing, though, she asked the most important question:

"How will we get into the town if they are looking for us?"

"We have no other option. Besides, we're hardly recognizable from those drawings."

The boy thrust the paper into his pocket and moved on with confidence.

Despite the fact that the station appeared to be deserted, there was a steam engine with carriages coupled to it, which was gleaming like new. Apparently Merula had been looking after it.

"The professor said that the Black Gnome sleeps during the daytime," Christopher whispered, then screwed up his left eye. "And it's daytime now."

"That's not quite what he said," Sophie replied in a whisper. "He said, 'It's daytime today.'"

"I thought that was a slip of the tongue."

The three travelers climbed carefully inside the engine. The cast-iron door of the coal box was locked. Loud snoring could be heard coming from behind it.

"I'm scared," admitted Sophie.

"The scent from the other side of that door isn't too promising. That's the smell of danger," Duke muttered very quietly.

On the count of three, the children leaned on the door. The dog pushed with his paws, too. The enormous hinges began to creak. At once, the snoring stopped.

With one eye closed, and clutching the cap in both hands, Christopher stepped into the opening. The pitch darkness swallowed him up straight away. The dim strip of light from the doorway couldn't dispel the gloom. The boy opened the eye that had been closed and, miraculously, saw a mountain of coal to the right with a shovel stuck in it, a wall in front of him, and a mat over to his left. The enormous fire-gnome was lying on it. His head was bald, and he had no beard at all. The sleepy corners of his eyes showed his annoyance: how dare this scoundrel interrupt his sleep?

Grumbling, the gnome got up and reached for his shovel. He didn't see Christopher at first. The boy took a deep breath, stepped forward and, with a swift movement, pulled the cap onto the giant gnome's head.

"Again! How much of this can I take?" the fire-gnome bellowed, and slumped back down onto the floor.

Plucking up her courage, Sophie peered inside. Duke poked his head in, too. Seeing that their opponent had been defeated, they opened the door wide.

"Why!?" the gnome howled.

"We need to get to the capital," the boy explained nervously.

He shot a sidelong glance at the door, ready to give his friends the signal to run at any moment.

"Don't you know any other way of making arrangements? The sort of thing that involves buying a ticket over there, handing in your luggage, tea and coffee, 'have a good journey,' and 'thank you very much'?"

"This is what we were told to do."

"Well you were taught wrongly! What I wouldn't do to be rid of that piece of cloth with its tassel. Some clever know-it-all appears every time. All they need to do is come and ask, 'Please would you take us, kind Merula.'"

"Kind?" the girl asked doubtfully.

"There's no one kinder on this side of the Chronos Stream." At that, the boiler-gnome gave a forced smile, which stretched all the way across his beardless face.

"Well we were told that you can't take a joke," the boy added, "and that you might hit us with your shovel. It's just in your nature."

"Lies! Take this cap off me!" the poor creature almost whimpered.

"Can't you take it off yourself?" asked Christopher.

"I can't. That's just the way it is."

"Then take us where we have told you," the boy ordered, in the kind of voice that would not take 'no' for an answer.

"I can't take you right into the town," the gnome muttered irritably. "So don't ask me to. And I'm not going to explain why. So there!"

He bent down, opened the firebox, and blew inside. A fire erupted from his jaws, sending sparks flying, and the coal in the very belly of the steam engine flared up, cheerily and hot. Then Merula tapped the manometer—a device for measuring the pressure of the steam—and wiped coal dust from the water-level gauge with his sleeve. Soon, the locomotive and the carriages coupled to it were traveling along the green plain.

"Reputation," the gnome began to philosophize out loud. It must be said that the cap made him look all the more terrifying, though a little ridiculous. "I have done so many good deeds in my life, I have transported so many people and others besides, and I have shoveled so much coal with these very hands! But all it took was for me to turn round at the wrong time, and hit that…what's his name…I forget…with the shovel. What was he doing poking his nose in everywhere anyway!? If he climbed into the cab, he wouldn't have been hit with the shovel. The bruise covered half of his face. So then he yelled: 'Put the pacifying cap on him! The pacifying cap!'"

"Didn't you try to explain what had happened?"

"To whom? No one ever listens to me. As soon as they see me, they run away. They say I have a bad reputation now. I had never heard that word before. I had to trek over to Temporus Certus to borrow a dictionary. He held the book very carefully out of the window to me. You can't expect him to come outside and shake hands now, the way old friends do."

"So was it you who left the cap with the professor?"

"I have no idea where he got it from. They're all over the place, those caps. They just hand them out willy-nilly."

"Who hands them out?" asked Sophie.

"The Ministry of Mumbles, Grumbles, and Other Rumbles," was the gnome's strange reply.

"We'll call in there and ask them to change their decision."

"Really? Are you trying to trick me? Because if you do, what will become of your reputation? It's already, well, you know…"

Merula tossed another piece of coal into the firebox and pulled a cord that was hanging above it.

There was a piercing whistle.

"What's the matter with our reputation?" Sophie asked again.

The gnome hesitated for a moment and then, from out of his pocket, he pulled a folded piece of paper exactly the same as the one the children had picked up on the platform.

"I don't know what you've done. It was none of my business until now. But they don't scatter leaflets like this all over the kingdom for nothing."

"You said no one would recognize us from those drawings," Sophie whispered to Christopher, poking him in the side with her finger.

"Doctor Doodle drew this," Merula went on, clearly welcoming the chance to talk after being alone for such a long time. "He's an incompetent bungler. But he's the only person here capable of even holding a brush. That's why he's the court artist."

Sophia glanced again at the drawing, which was more like a caricature, and then she frowned and sighed miserably.

Suddenly, they noticed a bright light again. The pendant came to life, and the voice that had read to them earlier now said:

"As hours and minutes race unrestrained,
Friends will be lost and enemies gained."

"Well," the black gnome said, leaning on his shovel and scratching the wrinkles on the back of his neck, "that is an ancient trinket. I have heard of such things, but never seen one."

He looked at his passengers with renewed interest.

Christopher carefully pulled his sword from its sheath. Instead of the pale glow, the blade now flared with a bright blue light. The children exchanged glances: they were moving in the right direction, but the meaning of this new message was horrendous. They would lose their friends and find enemies!

They didn't have a chance to think about all of this, though. The gnome was now chattering incessantly, talking about how he hated not only nightcaps, but all kinds of headgear. He even preferred to shave off his hair.

He gave another blast on the whistle. A tall, stone house appeared on the horizon. The train stopped in the middle of a field.

"We're here. I can't take you any further," said Merula, and he began to prod at the cap with his fat finger, but without touching it. "Take it off. You promised you would."

"Be careful," Sophie whispered into Christopher's ear, as she walked past him.

The boy waited until his companions were outside.

When only the two of them were left, Christopher prepared himself to run away at any minute, and carefully pulled the cap off the gnome's head. Immediately, his ears let out a whistling sound, thick white smoke streamed out of his nose, and he began to resemble a steam engine.

"Be careful," Merula said, imitating the girl's voice. "Gnomes have excellent hearing. It's strange you didn't know that. We have had centuries of practice. We've spent a lot of time underground, where it isn't always possible to see, but the tiniest rustle can be heard a long way off."

The boy became tense. He had never been so frightened. How could the professor have been so wrong about Merula's hearing? Meanwhile, the freed slave clutched his shovel even tighter with his muscly hands and…

…tossed some coal into the firebox.

The tension suddenly vanished.

"There is a hill further down there," the gnome said. "It has a long and gentle slope and leads directly to the gates of the town."

The boy was just about to wish him luck.

"There is something else," the giant gnome said hesitantly.

He took a portrait out of his breast pocket. On the piece of parchment, next to a much-younger Merula, stood a lovely lady gnome in a checked apron.

"Just in case you see her in town…Time has passed since then, of course, and she will have changed. Doctor Doodle painted this too, so you'll understand…but you should recognize her."

The gnome paused, shifting from one foot to the other, and then went on:

"She's called Marta. She should remember me."

"What shall I tell her?"

"Just say hello. Hello from Merula."

The boy leaped down. For a while, the fire-gnome watched as the three friends walked away, and then he put the engine in reverse. The smoke from the funnel of his engine soon disappeared over the horizon.

Chapter 6

The Prince Becomes a Slave

In the general pushing and shoving, no one paid any attention to the travellers as they made their way through the gate. But that didn't last long. Suddenly, one of the plump people selling bread rolls from a tray pointed in the direction of the young explorers and yelled at the top of his voice:

"Look! Who is that?!"

The crowd parted.

This is it now, Christopher thought. *We've had it. Now we'll be caught and put in prison, or perhaps worse…*

But something quite different happened.

"It's the prince!" cried the bread seller.

Dozens of townspeople rushed towards them, not angrily, but happily. Christopher felt encouraged. However, before he had time to rejoice, hundreds of hands and paws grabbed hold of…Duke, and began to toss him about!

"The patch! He has the patch! He has returned! The prophecy has been fulfilled!" voices cried from all around.

The dog's ears and tail kept reluctantly rising and being blown about in the wind. Christopher and Sophie were pushed onto the footpath. No one took any notice of them.

"It turns out that Duke is the prince," the girl said bitterly. "Not you."

"You're not a princess, either," the boy snapped back.

"I didn't really want to be one."

"An amber tail and a patch!" the excited townspeople cried in the meantime.

It was clear that Duke was very much enjoying it all. He was already being given gifts. A fluffy rug had been put beneath his paws, and a garland of flowers on his head, and some lady gnome was sprinkling his glossy fur with eau-de-cologne.

"That's Marta," Sophie said, tugging at Christopher's sleeve and looking at the picture Merula had given them.

A nice lady giant was gazing in awe at Duke. He had completely forgotten about his friends. Christopher and Sophie attempted to make their way through the plump bodies of the excited admirers and attract his attention. They even succeeded for a moment.

"I'm busy," he growled, and then reverted to his contented smile, bowing to his new adoring fans.

The girl called out the lady gnome's name, but all her attention was focused on the prince, and she didn't even turn round.

Christopher took Sophie by the hand.

"Let's go. There's nothing more we can do here."

With a sigh, the girl followed on behind her companion. Meanwhile, Duke was already being carried off somewhere, while a band played along.

The children paused for a moment next to a newspaper stand. "Four Years Without the Prince," read the headline on one of them. The article praised the wise leadership of Temporus Improbus, who worked every day for the prosperity of the kingdom, which had been abandoned at the whim of fate.

Underneath, there was a note saying that, due to the growing number of dissatisfied people, the Regent had ordered a threefold increase in the production of pacifying caps.

Suddenly, the children noticed that, beyond the triumphant procession as it moved away, someone was watching intently. He was standing in the shadows on the other side of the street.

"It's the professor," exclaimed the girl.

She was just about to run over to the man who looked like Temporus Certus, when the boy held her back.

"It's not him! Look at his hand. The left hand is just the same as the right. That's the Regent himself!"

Although he had suddenly lost his power and his subjects at the same time, Temporus Improbus didn't seem particularly concerned. He whistled something happily as he strode briskly down the street.

"Let's follow him," suggested Christopher.

They set off after the professor's brother as he walked along, glancing from time to time at his gold wristwatch. Christopher and Sophie could not possibly have known, but the highly polished face of the watch reflected the street behind the Regent very well, along with his two young pursuers.

When he reached the town hall with its huge clock tower, the Regent went inside. As soon as the children had slipped in behind him, the door banged shut! They found themselves in total darkness.

"My sword," the boy said, pulling it out.

Its bright red flame revealed a spiral staircase leading upward.

"You see, we are very close. It is time your pendant gave us some help, because I have no idea what to do next."

The girl held the stone in her hand and breathed on it. But nothing happened.

The staircase wound around a tall, motionless pendulum.

As the children climbed upward, they discovered a small platform from which there was an excellent view of the town. The Regent was standing, reading a newspaper next to a stained-glass window.

"Take a look at this," he said, as if nothing had happened. "It has just been printed on my orders."

The boy and girl froze in the doorway.

"Do come in."

Christopher held his sword in front of himself.

"Put down your weapon. I won't hurt you. I'm going to send you back home. Right now."

"Home?!" the girl exclaimed gleefully. "But how?"

"I'll send you to the past in the time machine. You will find yourselves in your own world, and will never see me, this town, or this kingdom ever again."

"A time machine?!" said Christopher, in a voice which contained notes of both delight and distrust. "But what about Duke?"

"The prince will stay here. Read this for yourselves."

The Regent held the paper out to them. It smelled of fresh ink.

The huge headline, which took up half of the page, read:

"The Prince, having returned after a long absence, has approved all the laws of our wise Regent, and appointed him Prime Minister."

Christopher lowered his sword in surprise. Then Sophie asked out loud:

"When did Duke find the time to appoint a prime minister?"

"He doesn't know it himself yet, but he definitely will. He won't be going anywhere. It's all to do with this spray," Temporus Improbus said, showing them a spray bottle. "One drop a day on the back of the neck, and he will remain as he has now become—slightly arrogant, a little lazy, and fond of flattery and small treats. A simple-minded ruler on the throne, who obeys my will and cares about nothing except his own pleasure, is just what I need. A pawn on the throne, and a powerful queen."

"But that's terrible!" the children exclaimed in unison.

"Just look, he's already enjoying this life. The infusion uses bamboo flowers. It's an ancient recipe. If only you knew how difficult it was to find the flowers."

The Regent beckoned to them and invited them to look out of the window. From the tower, they could see Duke sitting on the throne. One of his servants was scratching his ear, while he gladly accepted the gifts brought to him.

"But you've turned him into a slave," Sophie argued angrily, while Christopher held up his sword again and moved closer to her so that the blade would now protect them both.

"I thought you would have treated Merula differently. Yes, I know everything," laughed Temporus Improbus.

"I took the cap off his head. But if I had known that the gnome was harmless, I wouldn't have put it on in the first place."

"Oh, don't be so silly. You're not even from our world. Why should you care about what is going on here?"

"We care about any kind of injustice," the boy replied boldly. "Your brother believes that you are responsible for the kingdom's problems."

"My brother is stupid. He experiments with time himself, but he relies on the laws of physics when he should use magic. He will never succeed."

"That's not true," Sophia declared in desperation. "We saw how the hourglasses moved more slowly in a warm place than in the cold."

"Nonsense! That's because of the size of the grains of sand. They expand when they are heated. So a smaller quantity of sand will pass through per unit of time. How could he not understand that? Did you see his parrot? It's my brother's favorite pet. He thought that parrots could live forever. I proved the opposite."

Temporus Improbus chuckled.

"Now, he's constantly afraid of losing his friends. That's why he only associates with those who never grow old. The sturgeon, for example. He also has a tortoise."

"The professor told me how to defeat the gnome in a duel. That was magic."

"By closing one eye? That's an old trick. As soon as you close your eye, the pupil dilates. Then, when you open it again, your eye doesn't need any time to adjust to the darkness. How is that magic? And as for his hand, I was the one who made it age. It's just a shame that he only put his hand into the time machine. Otherwise, all of him would have been turned into an old man."

The professor's brother squinted nervously at the sword with its bright red flame, and slowly walked backwards. He soon reached a small, hidden door, opened it, and stepped into the dark corridor behind. They moved along in this way for a while, the tall, thin Regent retreating and the children watching him as they followed. It wasn't difficult to see that they were walking about inside a huge clock. There were sharp cogs all around, and a spiky trigger mechanism dangled above their heads. Eventually, they ended up in a semi-circular room.

"Well, you may care about injustice, but you have no choice now," the Regent finally spoke again.

"Is this your time machine?" asked Christopher.

"It certainly is. You are now standing at its very heart."

He opened another secret door and slipped out of the room. The mysterious contraption set in motion. The building shook.

"Everything is ready for the journey," his muffled voice called from behind the closed door. "You arrived here just under two days ago. Turn the wheel twice—it's in front of you—and it will send you exactly two days back into the past. Well, go on. Otherwise, you won't get out of here alive. I will lock you in here, and in a week or two I'll send a team of vultures to collect your bodies. You will starve to death. I promise."

Christopher and Sophie looked at each other. Tears were trickling down the girl's cheeks. It was clear that she didn't want to leave the dog.

"What should we do?" she whispered.

The boy didn't know what to say. He thought for a moment about how they hadn't been able to help Merula as they had promised, either.

"Come on, pendant, please tell us!"

Sophia placed the stone on her palm and breathed on it. But it was all in vain. The tears were now streaming from her eyes. They began to drip onto her hand and onto the stone itself. Then it finally happened. The pendant came to life! Its new words rang out under the roof of the old tower:

*"Dreaming of home, the heroes comprehend
that suddenly time will become their friend."*

The children looked at each other. Time would become their friend? They could only guess what that might mean.

"Hey! What are you doing in there?" Temporus Improbus called out in a worried voice from behind the door.

"Do as I told you, otherwise I will lock you in at once, and you won't be able to get out…"

But he didn't manage to finish what he was saying. Or rather, he did finish, but the children weren't listening. Christopher put his hand on Sophie's and together they turned the wheel…Once…

Chapter 7

A Trick

What does time travel look, sound and smell like? Many travelers describe it as flying down a kind of corridor. They can hear the hum of stars racing past. They see flashes of light, and there are bursts of sparks. The rapid flight causes dizziness and their ears pop. It smells of ozone, as if after a storm.

Neither Christopher nor Sophie had ever seen, heard or felt anything like it. It was all quite different. At first the cogwheels ticked softly, and there was a muffled chime in the distance. Billions of planets orbited their stars. Water trickled. Thousands of grains of sand brushed against the glass walls, which were close together. The smells kept changing.

This must be an aromatic clock. Parts of it are soaked in different scented oils, and a fuse or a stick is lit. As time goes by, it gives off one fragrance and then another, Sophie supposed.

Suddenly, all but one of the sounds stopped, and the children could hear it very clearly. They could each hear the beating of their own hearts. It was rather rapid, but nevertheless regular, like a clock.

Interesting, thought Christopher. *Is it possible to measure time with the beating of a heart? And how is this clock any worse than the others?*

The boy did not have time to finish thinking about this. The walls disappeared. They were standing in front of the professor's house.

"We did it!" exclaimed Christopher. "We've gone back one day! Your pendant gave us a timely clue: time will become our friend now. I was thinking that we should go back one day instead of two as well, but I couldn't decide whether I should tell you."

"And I wanted to suggest it, but I was afraid the Regent might hear. If you had tried to turn the wheel twice, I would have stopped you!"

Straight away, they noticed that the Forest of Chronos was not there. The land was covered with white flowers, which were beginning to wither.

Temporus Certus came out of the house. The children raced towards him and competed with each other to tell him about everything that had happened.

"…So Merula isn't dangerous at all," Christopher said at the end of the story.

"Now I see that I was mistaken and I did not treat him politely, when he had come to me for the dictionary. That is unforgivable! Scarcely had you sailed away when something unfortunate happened to the Forest of Chronos."

"It died," the girl said, nodding.

"Worse. It blossomed! Bamboo blossoms once every hundred years. And after that, it dies. The last time it happened, I was your age. So there was still plenty of time for the woods to grow and grow. And then this happened! I guessed it was the work of my brother. The time machine must be destroyed. But only after you have returned home, of course.

"We need to save the prince!" the girl said, grabbing the professor by the sleeve.

"Absolutely!" he replied. "If I had known what danger awaited you, I would never have let you go to the town on your own."

"We discovered from a piece of paper that they were looking for us."

Christopher pulled out of his pocket the leaflet they had picked up at the station. Now, though, it said something quite different:

DECREE!

Henceforth and until the end of the ages:

All the fleas in the kingdom are outlawed. The breeding and keeping thereof (either on the body or in any other place) is forbidden!

The use of perfume is prohibited. Everyone must smell as natural as possible, in order not to irritate the sensitive nostrils of the Prince.

A tournament has been declared in honour of the happy return of the sovereign

"That's it!" the professor said, interrupting the boy. "I will challenge my brother to a duel!"

"That makes no sense. Even if your teeth are sharper and your jaws are stronger than his," Christopher replied thoughtfully.

"It goes on to say," the girl piped up, "that the rules of the tournament are changing once and for all. From now on, there will be no duels. The competition will involve eating sugared bones in a certain amount of time."

The professor just shrugged his shoulders in astonishment.

"I have a plan," said Christopher. "We will play a trick on him."

It was impossible to hear what they talked about after that, but, a little while later, all three of them were in a boat being carried downstream with the current.

Merula was sleeping in his tiny room as before. There were branches of some sort strewn all over. It smelled of pine. When they woke him up, he barely moved. With an indifferent expression, he listened first of all to the children's story, and then to the professor's apology.

"We saw Marta," Sophie said at the end. "And we even tried to speak to her. But we didn't succeed. She works for the Regent. But there was no way we could get into the ministry. So we couldn't ask about the cap. But we need your help again."

The girl took hold of the gnome's hand in despair.

"I waited for a few hours, on a bench at the post office, for a letter from Marta. Then I went and cut down a branch...I should hand you over to the authorities. They might give me some kind of reward."

It was clear that the gnome was not saying this maliciously. The children also realized that there would be no reward for them.

"Anyway, you all...I would do better to go and chew some more juniper."

Merula reached for a bundle of green branches.

"It has an intoxicating effect on gnomes," the professor explained quietly.

"No, dear gnome," the girl said, clutching the giant gnome's hand more tightly. "We know that you are not bad. And Marta must know that. If you help us to save the prince, then you will become a hero! Everyone will love you again..."

"The Regent has declared a tournament," the boy said, showing the leaflet to the gnome.

"Will Marta be there?"

"The whole town will be there."

Merula tossed the juniper aside, scratched his wrinkly bald head, and held his broad hand out to Christopher.

As they were traveling on the train, the children told the professor about his experiment with the hourglasses.

"I know," he replied. "I sorted it all out myself. I had to talk to the Ant King straight away. It turns out that all objects expand when they are heated. It's just that we can't see it. But they can because they are tiny…As for the trick with the closed eye—I think you guessed that for yourself."

Instead of replying, the boy winked at the professor. Soon the town appeared on the horizon.

The site for the tournament had been set up opposite the town hall, next to a large fountain. It had been arranged like that for a reason. This was because a water clock was being used to measure time. First of all, two monkeys in uniform took some water from the fountain using a wide bowl inscribed with ancient hieroglyphs, and put it on a pedestal so that it was slightly higher than the identical vessel beside it. When the order was given, the one standing on the right pulled a stopper from the base of the upper bowl, and the water began to trickle down into the one below. The countdown had begun.

The competitors set about devouring the treats. They grunted and slurped excitedly. The crowds roared. Gnawed remnants flew into the baskets, which had been placed in front of each participant.

It was all managed by a herald dressed in colorful clothes.

"Time's up!" he shouted, as soon as the upper bowl was empty, and he waved a short wooden rod.

Everyone looked at the clock. The finished remnants were counted. A big-eared boxer called Lucky was the winner. Then the next contestants came out into the arena. The bowls were swapped around. The herald waved his rod once more, and everything began all over again.

Duke, who was surrounded by courtiers, was watching the proceedings attentively. In truth, he wasn't particularly excited. The dog's gaze seemed clouded. The Regent was nearby.

When the next stage was over, the herald again called for any contenders to come forward. Christopher and Sophie went out into the center. The monkeys immediately removed the boy's sword. Everyone stared in amazement at the children: why did these human beings, who were still very small, want to take part in the competition? They had no chance!

The herald grinned. Suppressed giggles could be heard coming from the crowd. Everyone fell silent, though, as soon as the children began to speak.

"I accuse Temporus Improbus of poisoning the Prince with nectar from bamboo flowers."

"And I accuse him of usurping authority," said Sophie.

In the silence that had fallen, these last words resounded particularly loudly.

"That's a lie! Put them behind bars!" shouted the Regent.

"It is true!" the voice of Temporus Certus called out.

He came out into the arena and stood next to the children.

The monkeys, who had been watching the vessels, grabbed hold of the professor. Everyone else, though, including the speechless herald, was now looking at the Prince. He merely yawned lazily. Apparently, the accusations that had been directed at the Regent did not trouble him in the slightest. Duke wearily climbed off his throne and made his way downward, as people gazed adoringly at him. He sniffed the children with a blank expression. Tears trickled from Sophie's eyes. She hugged the dog, put her arms around his head and began to whisper into his ear:

"What has he done to you! Do you really not recognize us at all? Remember how happy you were at the circus? Remember the smells there? At least remember the stench of the elephant manure! We were almost forced to clear it out!"

"I remember," the dog replied nonchalantly. "Arrest them."

He turned around and set off back to his place. Christopher realized that his plan—to tell the townspeople about the Regent's trick—would not work.

"I'm not done yet," exclaimed the boy, and stepped on the tail of one of the monkeys with all his might. The monkey howled. The professor pushed the other one away. Christopher snatched the rod out of the herald's hand and tossed it into the fountain.

"Fetch, Duke!" he called.

"Retrieve!" shouted the girl, who had just realized what was going on.

The dog's canine instincts took over. Duke ran after the stick and immediately disappeared into the jets of water. A moment later, soaked from the tips of his ears to the ends of his paws, he bounded back to Sophie and…began to lick her face, neck and hands. The dog's happiness was overflowing. He licked Christopher as well. Even the professor got to join in, as the dog gave his wrinkled hand a gentle, friendly nip.

"My brother!" Temporus Certus said, suddenly remembering himself.

The Regent had taken advantage of the general confusion and was already at the door of the town hall. They ran off after him. Duke fell behind straight away as his jubilant subjects were stroking and hugging him. The not-so-nimble professor also began to dawdle. So, when Christopher and Sophie ran into the tower, their friends were still with the crowd in the square.

The cogs began to turn: Temporus Improbus had reached the time machine first, switched it on, and hurried into the time travel room.

"Three days ago!" he said, puffing and panting, and taking hold of the wheel.

Suddenly a huge gnome hand landed on his shoulder.

"Try this on," boomed Merula's threatening voice.

It had been agreed that the gnome would wait in the tower for the Regent. In his free hand, he was holding the cap which, after overcoming his own fear, he had taken from Christopher.

However, he did not manage to put the hat onto the villain. Temporus Improbus pulled some kind of lever, and the whole room was flooded with a bright light. Merula squinted for a second, and in the moment of confusion, his opponent pushed him. The gnome managed to grab the

Regent by the sleeve, but then he tripped over the threshold and they both fell through the doorway. They flew down the stairs.

At that moment, the children came running.

"Quick. Into the room," the gnome called to them. "I'll hold him back."

The professor appeared on the stairs.

Christopher and Sophie didn't know what to do. The Regent managed to free himself and rushed back towards the time machine. The bulky Merula couldn't regain his balance on the stairs, and rolled even further down, landing at the professor's feet.

"Fly quickly!" they called from down below.

The Regent turned around and launched himself at the children. They did not even have time to shut the door. Together, they grabbed the wheel and started to count each turn together:

"One, two!!!..."

Christopher woke up and lifted his head off the table. A computer monitor was flickering in front of him. Outside the window, dozens of excited children were going with their parents from the circus. The show ended. A hot air balloon was swaying above the roofs of the houses next to the circus big top, as if nothing had happened. Just as before, jolly music could be heard coming from that direction.

The boy looked around in disappointment. Tears seemed to be streaming from his eyes: so had it all just been a dream?

The doorbell rang.

"There's a parcel for you, Christopher!" his mother called from downstairs.

The boy reluctantly went down. On the doorstep there was a long package with no return address.

"Dad must have ordered a present for you over the internet so that you're not too upset about the circus," his mother suggested.

He quickly peeled off the paper. Inside, there was a printed envelope and a sword. It was exactly the same as the one in his dream. Or had it really happened?

Christopher unsheathed the blade.

"It's glowing! Can you see it?" he exclaimed joyfully.

"Of course I can, my dear," his mother called after her son as he ran back to his room.

She just shrugged and said quietly, "Boys and their games!"

With trembling hands, Christopher opened the envelope, and all his doubts vanished. Inside, there was a letter.

Hello Christopher!

I am sending you your sword. I hope that you arrived home safely. Things are going well here in the Kingdom. We have dealt with my brother. We didn't even have to put the pacifying cap on him. He will be fine; he is working as a clockmaker now. Caps are now forbidden. Merula has become a hero. He proposed to Marta. The wedding will be soon. Duke remembers you often. He is setting up a town council. Some new, fair laws will be put in place. Even the Forest of Chronos has begun to grow back. But there's nothing frightening in there now. The townspeople go there to collect mushrooms and herbs.

Give my best regards to Sophia. And pay us a visit sometime, if you happen to come across another hot air balloon.

Your faithful friend,
Temporus Certus.

Christopher was reading the letter for the third time, when he heard a Skype alert. The name 'Sophie' popped up on the screen.

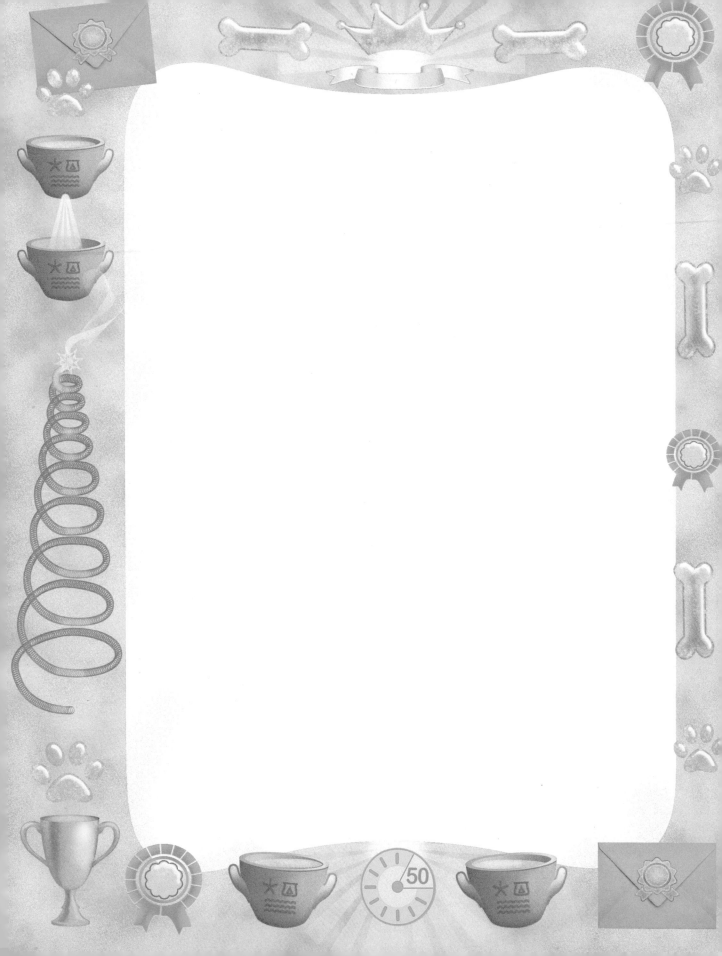

Made in the USA
San Bernardino, CA
21 June 2018